BiLLY *and the* BABY

Billy and the Baby

Tony Bradman & Lynn Breeze

PictureLions

An Imprint of HarperCollins*Publishers*

First published in hardback in Great Britain by HarperCollins Publishers Ltd in 1997
First published in Picture Lions in 1997

3 5 7 9 10 8 6 4
ISBN: 0 00 664611 5

Picture Lions is an imprint of the Children's Division, part of HarperCollins Publishers Ltd.
Text copyright © Tony Bradman 1992
Illustrations copyright © Lynn Breeze 1997
The author and illustrator assert the moral right to be identified as the author and
illustrator of the work.
A CIP catalogue record for this title is available from the British Library.
Printed and bound in Singapore by Imago.

Billy's mum was having a baby.

"It's growing inside me," she said.
"Just like you did, Billy."

So, that's why she's such a funny
shape these days, he thought.

Mum asked him if he wanted to feel the baby kick inside her tummy. Billy said he didn't mind.

"Can I have that box?" he said. Mum gave it to him.

Later, Billy was busy in his room. Dad knocked
on the door.

"I've got something to show you,"
he said. "We took lots of pictures
when you were a baby."

Billy wasn't all that interested,
but he looked at the album
to keep Dad happy.

"Can I have a picture?"
asked Billy. Dad gave
him one.

The next day Billy was drawing a picture, but Mum interrupted him.

"Would you like to see some of your old baby clothes?" she said. "Some might fit the new baby."

The clothes looked very small. They were all right for a baby, but Billy was glad he didn't have to wear things like that any more.

"Can I have this?" he asked. Mum said he could.

A few days later, Billy was looking in his box when Dad called to him. Billy sighed.

"Come and see what I've found," he said. "All your old baby toys." Dad got them out and played with them. Dads and babies might like them, but Billy didn't think they looked very exciting.

"Can I have this rattle?" he asked. Dad said he could.

At the weekend, Billy wanted to stick something on his box. But Mum said they had to go to the bookshop instead.

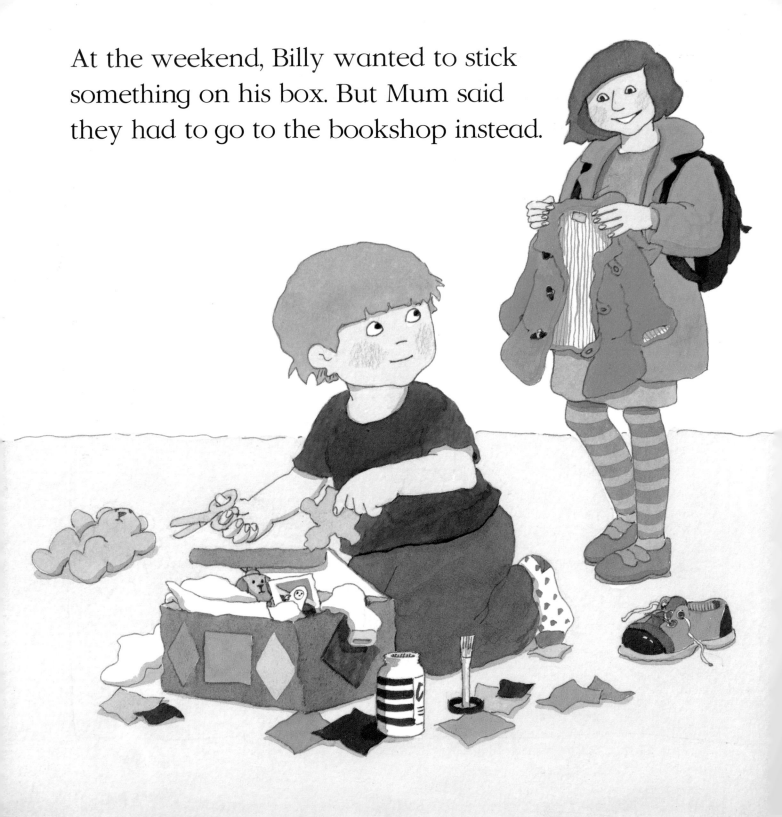

They bought lots of books… and all of them were about babies. Some of them were quite interesting. But most of them weren't.

"Can I have this one for my box?" he asked. It was an old book, one of his favourites. Mum said he could.

One afternoon, Dad said they had to go out. Billy wanted to work on his box, but he didn't make a fuss.

They went to the hospital where Mum was going to have the baby. They had a look round, and then they had to wait for a long time. It was very warm, and Dad dozed off.

"Can I have that?" asked Billy when they got home.
Dad said he could.

Billy had nearly finished the box when Mum asked him to help her.

"We're decorating the baby's room, Billy," she said. "And we don't want you to feel left out."

Billy was busy, but he didn't like to say no. So he helped Mum do some painting, and quite enjoyed himself in the end.

"Can I paint my box?" he asked. Mum said he could.

In the morning, Billy was sorting out all the things in his box when his Dad said he wanted to talk to him.

Dad explained that Billy might have to go and stay at Grandma's for the night when Mum went into hospital. He said they didn't want him to feel upset or worried about it.

"I'm not," said Billy. Dad looked surprised.
But Billy liked Grandma, and when he went
to visit her, she gave him a sweet.
   "Can I have another one for my box?" he said.
Grandma smiled.

Then one night, it happened.

Billy was woken by Mum and Dad. The baby
was coming, and they had to go to the hospital.

Mum and Dad did a lot of running about.
Mum was smiling, but Dad looked worried.

They took Billy to Grandma's on the way, and kissed him goodbye. Billy had his box with him.

It was ready now.

At breakfast the next morning, the phone rang. It was Dad.

"You've got a lovely baby sister, Billy," he said.
"She looks just like you, too!"

Billy was pleased, but he didn't want to talk for long. Dad's voice was very loud, and besides, he wanted to show Grandma what was in his box.

Later that day, Dad came back from the hospital.
He looked very tired.

"You mustn't think we won't love you any more
now we've got the baby," he said, and gave Billy
a big hug.

"Why would I think that?" said Billy. He was holding his box. "And when can I meet the baby?"

Dad took Billy to the hospital
the next day. Mum looked
very happy.

Billy looked at
his new baby
sister. He smiled.

"This box is for
you," he said.
"And all the
things inside
it are, too."

But the story doesn't end here.

Billy's baby sister soon grew up. She was a pain sometimes, but Billy loved her.

And as for the box…well, Billy's sister kept that.
It turned out to be very useful…